Corky & Nikita

A True Friendship

Henry Lee Barnes, Jr.

Illustrations: Julia Kushnirsky

HLB LOUDMOUTH PRODUCTIONS

Author photo by Francesco Valentino

Archway Publishing books may be ordered through booksellers or by contacting:

Archway Publishing
1663 Liberty Drive
Bloomington, IN 47403
www.archwaypublishing.com
1 (888) 242-5904

ISBN: 978-1-4808-2640-3 (sc)
ISBN: 978-1-4808-2642-7 (hc)
ISBN: 978-1-4808-2641-0 (e))

Print information available on the last page.

Archway Publishing rev. date: 02/09/2016

For my very brave and courageous sister, Brenda.

Nikita, a beautiful blue parakeet, lived in a pet shop with many other birds of all colors and sizes. One day, Nikita decided that she wanted to have an owner, one for herself. Someone, who'd take special care of her. And someone who would appreciate her sweet songs. Someone in need of a friend.

Nikita began to plan her great escape, but first, she must make her way through the large and crowded cage to say goodbye to all her friends.

"But how will you get out of here if no one comes to buy you?" asked one concerned bird.

"I won't wait for that," said Nikita, "I can't wait for that!"

"Look at us all. We've been in here for so long that we don't remember what it's like to fly about and enjoy the beauty of the world!"

Nikita wasn't exactly sure what she was saying, but it felt right to her. And some of the other birds seemed to nod their heads in agreement with her speech.

So, after long and careful thought, Nikita now knew what she must do.

On a warm afternoon, when the old shopkeeper came to feed the birds, upon opening the cage door, Nikita spread her pretty blue wings and flew past the startled man, as fast as she could fly! Out of the shop and up, up in the air she flew. She didn't dare to stop or look back, until she was certain that the building which she knew as her home was clear out of sight.

Flying high on the arm of the warm summer wind, the beautiful shades of blue in her soft feathers seemed to blend in with the sky that surrounded her. As she continued on her unknown journey, Nikita began to wonder what her new owner would be like. She knew that once she found him or her, they would instantly love her and take her in.

She would fill the house with music and good cheer. She would sing in the mornings and chirp sweetly and softly in the evenings. Well, chirp until the white blanket placed over the cage indicating the time to sleep, until the next day.

Although very new to this, Nikita knew that the owner and house had to be special. There must be a need for music, good cheer and friendship. You see, Nikita was that rare bird who could spread a good feeling all around her. Especially to those who didn't have it.

Gliding through the air Nikita felt so free and alive. She swooped upwards and then downwards like the daredevil airplanes in an air show. Her head was giddy with delight and she just went with the feeling. That is, until she began to feel an overwhelming sensation drawing her downwards to a house. The feeling did not frighten her, so she followed it to what she hoped would be her new home.

It was a quiet little town known as Markham. And it was truly beautiful to look at. Bubbling brooks, finely trimmed trees and even pebble roads adorned the town.

But the unusual feeling was coming from a big white house, off from the main road. It was beautiful to look at, with its tall columns and red roof. The red blossomed roses and colorful tulips, rocked gently in the summer breeze, as the sharply trimmed hedges stood firm, outlining the massive lawn. And the two giant water fountains, decorating both the front and back lawn, spouted cool water out of the mouth of a marble stoned angelic faced boy.

The fountain was too good to pass up after such an adventurous journey.

"Mmmmm, that's good," thought Nikita to herself. Losing her balance for but a brief second, poor Nikita fell backwards, smack in to the fountain! SPLASH was the only sound that echoed through the nearby bushes and trees!

The now soaked parakeet, felt a little silly, but soon realized just how good the water felt. She decided to make the most of it and have a bath, a bird bath. After the bath, Nikita shook and fluffed her feathers to dry off, and continued her search for her new owner.

Suddenly, a faint whimpering and sniffling was heard. It was as if someone had a cold or was crying. The sound was coming from a window on the second floor of the big white house.

So, without delay, Nikita spread her wings and flew up to the window's ledge, to see who was in the room. And to Nikita's surprise, it was a little boy lying in bed, sobbing.

"Poor little boy," a thoughtful Nikita said. "Whatever could be the matter?"

But the little boy did not see the pretty blue bird just outside his window looking at him.

So Nikita decided to sing to him. She began singing in her loveliest voice.

The boy stopped crying and slowly looked over to the window.

"A bird!" shouted the boy. "Oh boy, oh boy!" he said. After jumping up from the bed, he began to walk slowly over to the window, so as not to frighten the bird away. But he stopped short and grabbed at his stomach!

Nikita could see that he was in some kind of pain.

"What's the matter?" she asked.

"It hurts," said the boy. "Hey, you can talk!?" he shouted.

"Well, sure I can. But only to you," she answered. "Why were you crying?"

"Because my tummy hurts and mother said for me to stay in bed. But I want to go outside and play."

Nikita thought about the little boy and the nice home and she wanted to stay. So she added, "I could stay for a while and sing for you until you get better..."

"What is your name?"

"Corky. My name is Corky," said the boy.

"Mmmm... Corky. That's a nice name. My name is Nikita."

"Will you stay and play with me forever?" asked a very enthusiastic Corky.

"Sure I will. But I'm afraid that I will grow tired and hungry very soon because I've flown a great distance to find you."

"To find me?" said Corky. "Oh boy my own bird! Wait until I tell mother!" And Corky ran out of the room to tell his mother about his new pet and friend.

KUSHNIRSKY

Shortly after Nikita met the parents and the servants, a shiny new gold cage was setup for her in Corky's room. It had mirrors, toys, food and water inside. It even had a special door, one where Nikita could fly in and out, anytime she wanted.

"Wow! I'm going to like it here. My very own cage!" exclaimed a very excited Nikita. She had been used to sharing a cage with many other birds. Most of them were her friends, but still, it did feel a bit cramped at times.

Days passed, and Corky and Nikita were inseparable. They spent every hour together, from morning to night. Now that the pains in Corky's stomach were gone, caused by too many cookies from Cook, Nanny and Charles, the butler, the two could enjoy each other's company without worry. It had fast become a pure and solid friendship between boy and bird.

Corky was very happy to have Nikita as his friend and pet, because he had no brothers or sisters to play with. And both his parents were just too busy to spend much time with him. Instead, he would often pester Charles or Nanny to play ball or chase after him on his tricycle. Or often playing with the fruit & vegetables that Cook gave him, make believing it was a real person.

But something beyond his or Nikita's control, loomed over them like a dark cloud. This something caused Corky to become very silent one day, sullen, even. Nikita was bathing and singing playfully, when she noticed the change over her friend.

"What's the matter Corky?"

He lowered his head before answering. "Soon I will have to start school and we won't be able to play together."

"Sure we will. We can play when you get home." said a practical Nikita.

"But I don't want to go to school. I won't know anybody there." Corky said very unhappily.

"Oh you'll meet lots of new people and make many new friends!"

And she was right.

After just three days at school, Corky had many new friends. Every day, he would come home with one to play and they'd have milk and cookies. Soon, they'd go outside and hardly see much of Nikita at all. One day, while playing with his friend Tim in Corky's room, Nikita felt a bit left out. So she began to sing loudly for attention. This prompted Corky to shout at her to be more quiet!

Another time, while coloring with his friend Judy, Nikita started flying and singing all over the room. She went so far as to land on Corky's shoulder, which really bothered him.

"What a pest you are today Nikta!" yelled the boy. And with that, he put her back in the cage and locked the door. The little bird's feelings were really hurt by this and she thought perhaps Corky didn't like her any longer and wished her gone.

Later that night, she found it difficult to sleep. She wondered what she would do if he indeed wanted her to go away. He meant the world to her now and wanted to stay. She would talk with him in the morning. Now she stretched out her wings, yawned and fell asleep.

Unfortunately, the morning found her too late, for she had over-slept. And Corky was already off to school. He left without saying 'goodbye'. Her heart sunk and she knew what she must do, regretfully...

Later that afternoon, Corky came running in to the room to show off his new fire truck to Nikita. He had traded his model car for it with Robert. He first looked in the cage, then around the room, but she wasn't there. Perhaps the fountain out back, he thought, only to find her not there either. He began to get upset and ran to the house to question the staff of her whereabouts.

"I'm afraid I have not seen your little feathered friend today," said Cook.

"Nor I." added Nanny.

"Do you mean that she is gone? How upsetting this must be for you!" said Charles. "But why would she leave her beautiful home, when she has everything that a bird could want? And she loves you so."

"I don't know why she left. I haven't really played with her lately and she bothers me when I'm playing with my real friends." admitted Corky.

"Your _real_ friends" sir? I thought Nikita was your real friend." asked Charles with a raised eyebrow.

"Oh she is! She is my real friend! I miss her and I want her to come back," sobbed Corky!

"Perhaps Master Corky has just answered his own question. You must treat all your friends the same way. Just because Nikita is a bird, does not mean that she doesn't have feelings too. Just like you and I," said Charles.

Corky thought for a moment. "You mean I hurt her by not talking or playing with her?"

"I'm afraid so." He said.

"Oh gosh, I'm so sorry. I wish she was here so that I could tell her," sobbed Corky even harder than before.

"I know you do," said Charles as he pulled a white handkerchief out of a top pocket and dried the boy's face.

That night Corky refused dinner with his parents and excused himself to his room. He was feeling so low and took to his room. Cook prepared a tray to be sent up to his room, but he had no appetite. The boy could only lay in bed thinking of the good times he and Nikita had before school started and when she first came to him.

And as suddenly and unexpectedly as that time, Corky heard music from outside his window. He jumped up and ran to the window to see.

"Nikita, Nikita! You've come back!" shouted a very happy Corky.

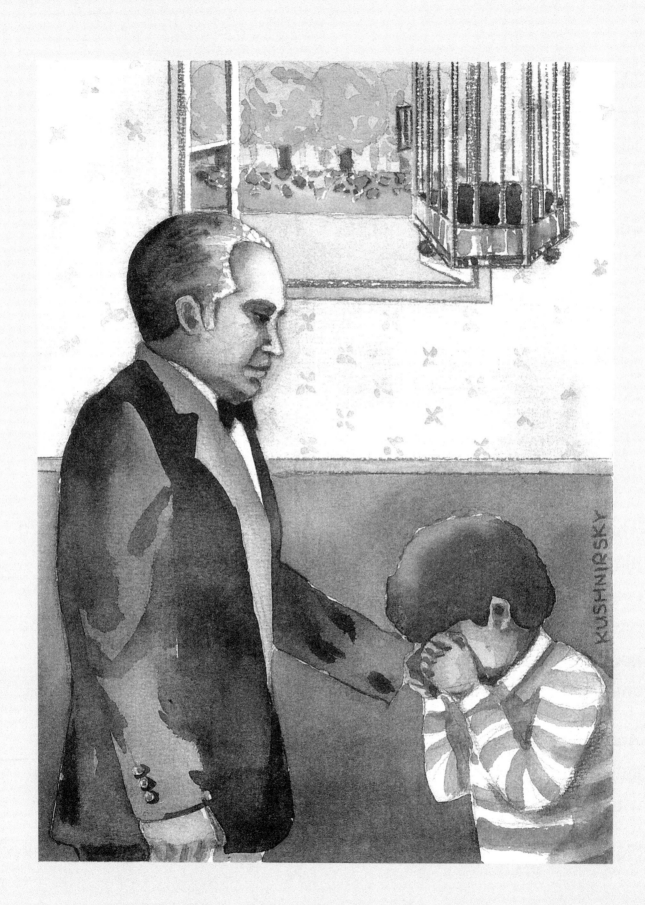

And there she sat, looking in at her best friend's tear stained face, chirping sweetly.

"Oh Nikita, I'm so glad you're back. But why, why did you leave?"

"I thought you wanted me to go away" said a relieved Nikita.

"Oh no, I want you to stay forever and ever!"

"Good, because that's how long I want to stay here with you. Forever and ever!"

And from that moment on, Corky treated Nikita just like the good friend that she was!

The End

CPSIA information can be obtained
at www.ICGtesting.com
Printed in the USA
LVOW05*2340171017

552830LV00018B/265/P